MW01098144

Copyright 2019
Illustrations copyrighted 2019

All rights reserved. No part of this publication may be reproduced,
Distributed, or transmitted in any form or by any means, including
Photocopying, recording, or
other electronic or mechanical methods, without the prior written
permission of the publisher, except in
the case of brief quotations embodied in critical
reviews and certain other noncommercial uses
permitted by copyright law.

Dedication

We dedicate this book to our son and to all of the special angels in our lives. Thank you for your love, support, and encouragement.

Alejandro, you are an inspiration to many, and your uniqueness is a blessing to us all. We love you more than bacon. Always, Momma & Dadda

Alejandro and the BACON Breakfast

Written By Claudia and Chris Diaz

Illustrations By Debbie J Hefke

Good Morning, **Alejandro**.

Give mommy a kiss.

It's time for school.

Time to get up.

You know what to do.

Let's make it quick. We don't want to be late.

Alejandro, hurry up and pick a plate.

Do you want french toast piled sky high?

OR how about some delicious pancakes with a blueberry side?

NO, NO, NO, bacON.

Let's try to compromise.

How about scrambled eggs with bacon for our

morning feast.

Mommy can make it quick and

especially neat.

BACON?

ALEJANDRO! Stop running, and put the tablet down.

Let's use your words and make a sound. Your belly is empty,

and we are so late. Mommy wants to know now what you want

on your plate!

You don't want french toast. You don't want pancakes.

You won't eat scrambled eggs with bacon.

So, what is left to fill your belly?

How about tortillas with a side of jelly?

Bacon?

Please, with a cherry on top!

Alejandro, let's get serious.

You are making mommy delirious.

You can't go off to school without a good breakfast.

Now, let's sit down and settle this.

I have cooked pancakes and french toast.

Don't forget scrambled eggs with bacon.

I swear, it's not a boast.

The tortillas and jam were delicious, but maybe,

just maybe, we should try plain toast.

Oh, look, **Alejandro!** Here comes dad.

I am sure he would be happy to know what you've had.

Quick! Take a bite of something new,

so he can watch you **chew, chew, chew!!!**

Good Morning, **Alejandro**.

Give daddy a hug and a kiss.

Oh, my goodness!

Who could have dreamed of a breakfast like this?

It looks absolutely the best!

I am beside myself looking at all of your options.

Alejandro, please stop spinning,

and let's try something new.

I see tortillas and jelly, french toast piled high, a stack of pancakes with a blueberry side.

I see scrambled eggs with bacon lovingly prepared.

If you want to practice making friends, Alejandro, it would be nice if you'd share. Mommy and daddy love you so much.

Now, let's sit down and eat this huge brunch.

Even with all the food prepared with love and care...

Maybe, just maybe, your craving has been declared.

Yes, bacon is your one and only breakfast wish, so it will be

cooked up quickly in hopes that you will enjoy it.

Alejandro, we know you like bacon.

You ask for it every day.

We accept that your taste is limited now,

and that is OKAY.

We will continue to explore other options for your dish.

Now, let's sit down and enjoy your breakfast wish.

LOVE THAT **BACON!**

31131384R00020

Made in the USA
San Bernardino, CA
02 April 2019